C.1

☞ **W9-CFD-279**

	DATE DUE		
MAR 19 '03			
MAR 26 '03			
APR 2 '03			
MAR 4 '03			

C.1

E
WAT

Waterstone, Rachel.

Who's under
grandma's quilt?

GERTRUDE C FOLWELL SCHOOL
MOUNT HOLLY, NEW JERSEY

WHO'S UNDER GRANDMA'S QUILT?

by RACHEL WATERSTONE
illustrated by VIRGINIA ESQUINALDO

FIRST STORY

First Story Press

To Jason, Shani, and Julie, with love —R.W.

To all children, and with much love to Henry —V.E.

Text copyright ©1997 by Rachel Waterstone
Illustrations copyright ©1997 by Virginia Esquinaldo

First Edition

First Story Press
Corinth, Miss.   St.Louis, Mo.
1-888-754-0208

Cataloging-in-Publication

Waterstone, Rachel.
  Who's under Grandma's quilt / author, Rachel Waterstone;
illustrator, Virginia Esquinaldo.
  p. cm.
  Preassigned LCCN: 97-60090
  1-890326-08-9
  SUMMARY: The search is on for who's hiding under Grandma's
quilt, with the animals working in cooperation with one another
except for one tattletale piglet.

I. Title
PZ7.W384Wh 1997   [E]
                               QB197-40370

Printed in Hong Kong

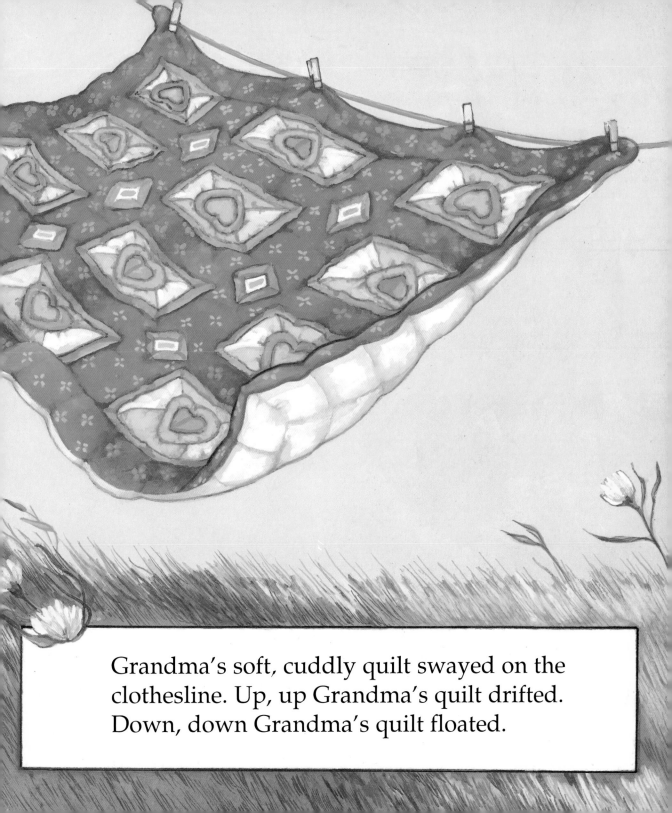

Grandma's soft, cuddly quilt swayed on the clothesline. Up, up Grandma's quilt drifted. Down, down Grandma's quilt floated.

Up, up the quilt drifted. Suddenly the breeze snatched Grandma's quilt so high the clothespins popped! Down, down the quilt floated and landed on the soft, grassy ground.

Then the quilt moved! A bump and a lump that thumped giggled under Grandma's quilt.

Baby chick darted from the farmyard.
"Who's under there?" he peeped.

The bump spoke in a sweet little voice,
"Can you lift the quilt and get me out?"

"You better not!" oinked curly-tailed piglet racing from the barn. "That's Grandma's quilt, and you better not bother it. If you do, I will tell Grandma."

"Go tell Grandma," peeped baby chick. "I want to help."
But he could not lift the quilt by himself.

Baby chick peeped to the quilt, "Follow me. I will find someone to lift the quilt."

And the quilt, with a bump and a lump that thumped, followed baby chick's peeps.

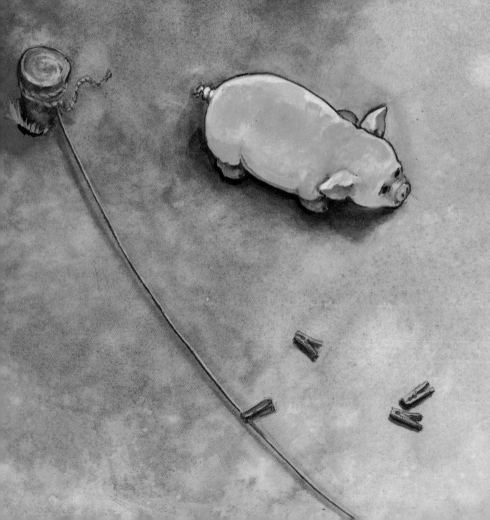

"Are you talking to someone under Grandma's quilt?" meowed long-whiskered kitten playing in her basket on the porch.

"I'm talking to a bump," peeped baby chick.

"And to me, too!" announced the lump that thumped in another little voice.

Baby chick peeped to long-whiskered kitten, "Can you lift the quilt?"

"You better not," oinked curly-tailed piglet. "If you do, I'm going to tell Grandma."

"Well, go tell Grandma," replied long-whiskered kitten as she tried to lift the quilt. The quilt, however, was too heavy. "Follow me," she said.

So the quilt, with a bump and a lump that thumped, followed the voices of long-whiskered kitten and baby chick to find help.

"Who's under Grandma's quilt?" asked floppy-eared puppy with his tiny bark.

Baby chick peeped, "We don't know. Can you lift Grandma's quilt so we can find out?"

"We should help," meowed long-whiskered kitten.

"You better not bother Grandma's quilt," oinked curly-tailed piglet. "If you do, I will tell Grandma."

Floppy-eared puppy shook his ears. "We can't lift it by ourselves. Follow me."

So the quilt, with a bump and a lump that thumped, followed the voices of floppy-eared puppy, long-whiskered kitten, and baby chick.

"Whom are you talking to under Grandma's quilt?" honked wiggly-necked goose.

"Can you lift Grandma's quilt so we can find out?" peeped baby chick.

"We should help," meowed long-whiskered kitten.

"We can't lift it by ourselves," said floppy-eared puppy.

"If you bother Grandma's quilt, I will tell Grandma," oinked curly-tailed piglet.

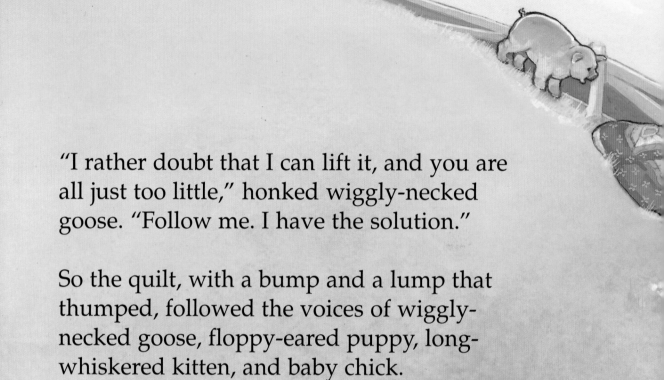

"I rather doubt that I can lift it, and you are all just too little," honked wiggly-necked goose. "Follow me. I have the solution."

So the quilt, with a bump and a lump that thumped, followed the voices of wiggly-necked goose, floppy-eared puppy, long-whiskered kitten, and baby chick.

They found prancing pony under a big oak tree.
"Who's under Grandma's quilt?" he neighed.

Baby chick peeped as loud as he could, "Can you
lift Grandma's quilt so we can find out?"

"We should help," meowed long-whiskered kitten.

"We can't lift it by ourselves," said floppy-eared puppy.

"They are just too little," honked wiggly-necked goose.

"You better not," oinked curly-tailed piglet. "You should not bother Grandma's quilt."

Prancing pony neighed to curly-tailed piglet, "Don't be silly. Grandma would want us to help. Now everyone grab a corner and lift!"

Up ... up sailed the quilt!

Out jumped the bump and a lump that thumped.

"It's Grandma's girl!" merrily shouted the bump.

"And it's Grandma's boy!" squealed the lump that thumped.

Once again Grandma's quilt landed on the soft, grassy ground. Then the quilt moved! A very oinky voice shouted, "Can you get me out of here?"

"Oh no!" peeped, meowed, barked, honked, neighed, and shouted the others.

"We better not bother Grandma's quilt," sang Grandma's girl pretending to leave. "We better tell Grandma."

So Grandma's girl led the parade around the quilt as they pretended to leave.

"Wait!" oinked the voice from under the quilt. "Don't you want to help who's under Grandma's quilt now?"